Little, Brown and Company

Hachette Book Group
1290 Avenue of the Americas, New York, NY 10104
Visit us at lb-kids.com

Little, Brown and Company is a division of Hachette Book Group, Inc.
The Little, Brown name and logo are trademarks of Hachette Book Group, Inc.

The publisher is not responsible for websites (or their content)
that are not owned by the publisher.

First Edition: October 2014

Library of Congress Control Number: 2014940697

ISBN 978-0-316-28360-1

10 9 8 7 6 5 4 3 2 1

WOR

Printed in the United States of America

# Ever After High™

# THE HAT-TASTIC TEA PARTY PLANNER

By Melissa Yu

*This party will be tea-riffic!*

L B

LITTLE, BROWN AND COMPANY
NEW YORK  BOSTON

Charm blossom, milkflower, spritzle-fizzle tea, a time as delightful as carnivals with thee!*

*Riddlish translation: Tea parties rock!

Madeline Hatter loves a good party, and she knows the most wonderlandiful ones involve a good kettle of tea. After all, she aspires to one day own a Tea Shoppe just like her father's in the Village of Book End! Maddie is always ready to throw a tea party—she has all the main supplies stocked in her Hat of Many Things.

Want to throw your own tea party that is as epically hexciting? Your Ever After High BFFAs (best friends forever after) are here to take the riddles out of throwing a hat-tastic soiree, with ideas for food, games, activities, and, of course, tea!

# Time to Spellebrate!

**Raven:** Before you put the cup before the kettle and get too far into planning a tea party, you should decide what time of day to hold it and how long it will be.

**Maddie:** I think two to three hours in the evening is hat-tastic.

**Lizzie:** Off with your head! Erm . . . I mean, I like to hold my parties in the morning. Mmmm . . . Tea with buttery breakfast pastries is just divine! Dwarven doughnuts, merry muffins . . . and then a game of croquet afterward!

**Maddie:** Remember how in Wonderland our tea parties were always so much?

**Kitty:** Hex yeah! So much muchness is the only way to do anything, especially a tea party! I remember all the page-ripping outfits everyone wore, too!

**Maddie:** Like my inside-out and upside-down blue-and-green feather gown! That's what I'm going to wear to Apple's tea party next week!

Maddie . . . that sounds so Wonderland! But I think you would look lovely in a classic party dress, with lacy white gloves and sparkly accessories. We're going to eat all the traditional savory foods, like Fairy Finger Sandwiches, and sweet treats, such as my Critter Cupcakes.

So...no feather gown?

Well . . . um . . .

As you can see from Apple and Maddie's discussion, having a theme will help you work out all your hexquisite party details, down to your decorations, snacks, and party favors, and then your guests will know what to hexpect!

What will your theme be? How will you let your guests know about it? What kinds of tea and snacks will you serve? You can brainstorm your ideas starting on page 44. If you can't think of all the details now, read on for a fairyload of suggestions!

# An Epic Invite!

Invitations are the prologue of every party. My friends and I like to add our personal touch to them. I love putting my creative skills to use and painting my invites!

*Cedar*

## You're Invited to Tea!

To: _____

From: _____

When: _____

Where: _____

RSVP by: _____

## You're Invited to Tea!

To: _____

From: _____

When: _____

Where: _____

RSVP by: _____

One time, I sent out invites shaped like smiles that disappeared once they were read, but then I followed them up with hext messages as reminders.

*Kitty*

I've added messages in Riddlish on my teapot-shaped invitations...sometimes not on purpose....

*Maddie*

## YOU'RE INVITED TO TEA!

To: _____

From: _____

When: _____

Where: _____

RSVP by: _____

MirrorVite is the best! It's a MirrorPhone app that lets me choose from design templates, so I can send out my invites as fast as I can run!

Cerise

Hexts                                    Rewrite

# You're Invited to Tea!

To: _____

From: _____

When: _____

Where: _____

RSVP by: _____

You're Invited To Tea!

To: _____

From: _____

When: _____

Where: _____

R.S.V.P. by: _____

I like to cut out mirror frames from black construction paper, glue them to purple paper, and then elegantly hand-letter them.

Raven

# A Fablelous Table

Back home, the castle dwarves always make sure our royal table is properly set for afternoon tea. Sometimes the woodland creatures help out, too. Everything always looks so perfectly splendid!

*Apple*

Don't tell Apple, but sometimes it can be hat-tastic to set the table for a traditional Wonderland tea—which means anything goes! When I set the tables at the Tea Shoppe, sometimes I'll stand on my head and close my eyes. It's always so so so so so so so delightful to see what happens!

*Maddie*

# A Royal Place Setting

# Shape-Shifting Napkins
## The Queen's Heart

Lizzie

My favorite shape to fold my red napkins into is the heart, of course!

YOU CAN USE EITHER A RED PAPER NAPKIN OR A CLOTH ONE, AS LONG AS IT IS SQUARE.

1. Lay the napkin flat on a table. The side you want as the front of the heart should be facing down.

2. Fold the bottom corner up to the top corner, forming a triangle.

3. Take the left corner and fold it up to meet the top of the triangle. Repeat with the right corner. You should now have a square.

4. Tuck about a third of the tip of each of those corners into the napkin.

5. Flip the napkin over carefully.

6. Fold the back of the napkin down so you can't see it from the front.

7. Flip the napkin over again.

8. Tuck in the top points until they're round.

9. Place a heart on the plate at each table setting.

1

2    3

4

5

6

7+8    9

13

# Shape-Shifting Napkins
## A-Tisket, A-Tasket,
## A Fancy Napkin Basket

You'd be surprised how a sturdy basket holds up during a run in the woods! Napkins folded into baskets are also a good way to present your guests with beef jerky--or sweets, if that's what your guests like--at the table. My friends flipped their hood when they first saw these!

*Cerise*

YOU CAN USE EITHER A PAPER NAPKIN OR A CLOTH ONE, AS LONG AS IT IS SQUARE.

**1** Lay the napkin flat on a table.

**2** Fold the bottom corner up to the top corner, forming a triangle.

**3** Fold the bottom of the triangle up about three inches.

**4** Flip the napkin over so the fold is on the back.

**5** Turn the napkin right so the triangle is facing left.

**6** Fold the top corner down until it's two inches from the bottom corner.

**7** Fold the bottom corner up until it's two inches past the top fold.

8 Tuck the two inches behind the napkin. Your napkin basket should be pointed at the top and flat at the bottom.

9 Fold the pointed top layer down the front of the basket, and then fold the pointed bottom layer down the back of the basket.

10 Straighten the edges and open the basket to stand it up.

11 Add a treat inside the basket, and put it at a place setting!

# Shape-Shifting Napkins
## The Mad Hatter's Bow Tie

I like to fold my napkins into bow ties. They're fairy pretty and they're practical! You never know when you'll need to dress up a white rabbit!

*Maddie*

YOU CAN USE EITHER A PAPER NAPKIN OR A CLOTH ONE, AS LONG AS IT IS SQUARE.

1. Lay the napkin flat on a table. If the napkin is printed on one side, that side should be facing down.

2. Fold the top side down and the bottom side up to meet in the middle.

3. Again, fold the top and bottom sides to meet in the middle.

4. Fold the left side one-third of the way right.

5. Fold the right side left to overlap.

6. Turn over the napkin, and cinch it in the middle.

7. Tie a ribbon around the middle to secure your bow tie.

8. Place a bow tie napkin on the plate at each table setting.

1

2

3

4

5

6+7

# Fairy Fun Fans

*Cerise*

Drinking hot tea and wearing my hood and cloak leaves me in a big bad bind: How do I stay cool? Luckily, my grandmother taught me how to make this totally wicked fan out of a piece of paper!

## Paper Fans

You can use any color or type of rectangular paper—I usually glue a piece of purple construction paper onto a piece of red paper so my friends can choose whether they want to be more Royal or more Rebel. Fold the narrow side of the paper about a half inch. Turn the paper over, and fold the paper another half inch. Continue to fold the paper in this accordion style until you reach the other end. Holding the folded paper at one end, tie a ribbon or a piece of yarn—again, red for Royal or purple for Rebel!—around it to hold it in place.

I think it's a purr-fect idea to drink hot tea while basking under a bright sun, but a fan can come in handy to hide my smile when I can't stop grinning! I like to decorate my paper with kitty paw prints and add beads to the ribbon for a hextra-special touch!

# A Tea-riffic Selection

Maddie

Earl Grey and I love going into the Enchanted Forest and finding ingredients to make new flavors of tea for my father's Tea Shoppe! Charm blossoms, chrysanthemums, phoenix feathers, dragon scales...you never know what the tea will taste like until you mix them up!

My friends till The End all have their favorite types of tea, so I keep those tea bags stocked in my Hat of Many Things in case we have an impromptu tea party. Apple, of course, enjoys Cinnamon Apple White Tea. Cerise always goes for Earl Grey-Wolf Tea. (Oh, don't worry, Earl Grey! You're not in the tea!) Kitty likes Kiss the Green Frog Tea. Cedar's favorite is still a riddle to me. She definitely runs away when I tell her I'm making Wood-Fired Berry Tea, though! I wonder why....

## WHICH TEA ARE YOU DESTINED FOR?
## TAKE THIS SHORT QUIZ TO FIND OUT!

1. It's lunchtime! Where would we find you in the Castleteria?
   a. With your usual crowd of BFFAs, of course.
   b. Wherever there's an open seat—you're comfortable with both the Royals and the Rebels.
   c. Scarfing down your lunch—you want to fit in that beginners' archery lesson.
   d. At the table of your choice—your friends will sit where you sit.

2. What's your favorite item in your closet?
   a. the most gorgeous pair of heels ever after
   b. a comfortable jersey tunic, preferably with a fun pattern such as hearts
   c. your trendy and broken-in jeans—stylish and comfy for all your activities!
   d. a shiny tiara fit for a queen

3. How many times do you hit snooze before getting up in the morning?
a. Once. You just want to see if Prince Charming comes to the rescue in your dream.
b. Twice. A few more minutes of sleep won't set you back.
c. None. You have so much to do, and there's not a minute to waste!
d. What snooze button? You don't need an alarm clock to tell you to wake up.

4. What are your plans for the weekend?
a. Shopping with your friends.
b. It's a toss-up. You might go to a friend's house, or you might curl up with a good book.
c. You've been dying to try the new rock-climbing gym, but you'll have to fit it in between your volunteer work and your singing lessons.
d. A day at the spa, complete with a mani-curse and pedi-curse.

5. How would your BFFAs describe you?
a. the cheerleader
b. the reliable friend
c. the go-getter
d. the trendsetter

### IF MOST OF YOUR ANSWERS ARE:

 **A** Your go-to tea might be orange tea! Like Ashlynn Ella, you are sweet and full of life. You are optimistic, and your glass is always half full. You're always surrounded by your friends, who think you're tons of fun to be with.

**B** The subtle flavor of green tea might suit you best! Like C.A. Cupid, you're easy to get along with, and your BFFAs go to you when they need sensible advice or a shoulder to cry on. You enjoy hanging out with your friends, but you'd be perfectly satisfied spending some time alone.

**C** You should try oolong tea, which has a robust flavor. Like Briar Beauty, you're adventurous and like to try new things. You like being outdoors, and you always have a packed schedule.

 **D** White tea will suit your elegant tastes. You are sophisticated and a confident hard worker. Like Apple White, you are the leader of your group of friends, and your classmates look up to you.

# Simply Royal Cupcakes

My songbird friends love to hang around the table of my tea parties because they think the crumbs of my cupcakes are royally delicious. I bake simple vanilla or chocolate cupcakes in mini-muffin tins, then add toppings that remind me of my best friends forever after! I like to take a container of white frosting and add red food coloring until the frosting matches the color of my dress!

*Apple*

For one of Maddie's tea parties, I cut out top hats from colorful construction paper and pasted pictures of us or our friends onto it, then stuck one into each cupcake. Maddie called them legendary—at least I think she did. She was speaking in Riddlish!

## Cupcake Toppers

- pictures of your favorite EAH students
- toothpicks
- tape

1. Punch out the cupcake toppers at the back of the book.
2. Tape a toothpick to the back of each topper.
3. Stick each topper into a cupcake.

TIP: Personalize them! You can also cut out and use pictures of you and your tea party guests.

Sometimes I'll make frostings of different flavors. For one party, I made cupcakes with this orange frosting that was spelltacular!

## Orange Buttercream Frosting

- 1 cup butter, softened
- 4 cups confectioners' sugar
- ½ cup orange juice
- 1 small orange (optional)

1. Using an electric mixer, beat the butter in a large mixing bowl. Slowly add the confectioners' sugar one cup at a time to the bowl, and beat the mixture until it is combined and nice and fluffy.

2. Add the orange juice, then continue to beat until the frosting is smooth.

3. Spread the frosting on the cupcakes with a butter knife, and top each with a thin slice of orange, for decoration (optional).

# Fairy Finger Sandwiches

Kitty

I think Fairy Finger Sandwiches are a must for a spellbinding spread at a tea party. And the best choice is obviously tuna salad. Drain a seven-ounce can of tuna, and mix it together with a creamy salad dressing, like ranch. Then add about a tablespoon of sweet pickle relish, and mix. Plop it between two slices of bread, then cut the sandwich into four squares. Tuna is delicious!

Apple

*Blech!* Tuna? I much prefer a Brie and apple sandwich.

Kitty

Sigh. Of course you do.

Apple

Ahem. To make this sandwich, spread mayo onto two slices of bread. On one slice, place a small bit of Brie and a thin piece of apple. Then place the second slice of bread on top. Cut off the crusts and then cut the sandwich into four neat squares.

That's so . . . simple. . . . I think tuna salad is much better! What do you think, Cerise?

Um, I think it's a good recipe, Apple. But I'd add a little ham to go along with the Brie and apple. Mmmm . . . meat!

Kitty

Cerise

# Masterpiece
# Blueberry
# Scones

Last summer, when Raven Queen and her father, the Good King, came to visit me and my dad, they brought along these scones, which were so epically delicious we went all whale on them and devoured them! Honest to goodness! And Raven, being her totally not-evil self, shared the recipe.

*Cedar*

## Makes 8 scones

### Ingredients

- 3 cups all-purpose flour
- ⅓ cup granulated sugar
- ½ teaspoon salt
- 5 teaspoons baking powder
- 1 egg, beaten
- 1 cup milk
- ¾ cup butter, melted
- ¾ cup fresh blueberries

26

## Directions

1. Preheat the oven to 400 degrees Fahrenheit.

2. Use nonstick spray to coat a baking sheet

3. In a large bowl, combine the flour, sugar, salt, and baking powder.

4. In a small bowl, mix together the egg and milk.

5. Add the butter and the mixture into the large bowl, stirring until well blended.

6. Add the blueberries and stir lightly until they're evenly spread out in the dough.

7. Spread flour on a clean counter or cutting board.

8. Transfer the dough onto the floured surface, and knead it a little and form it into a flat circle about a half inch thick.

9. Cut the circle into eight pieces by slicing it into quarters, and then cutting each quarter in half.

10. Place the dough slices onto the baking sheet. Bake for 15 minutes, or until the top is golden brown.

Serve the scones with butter or jam!

# Fablelous Green Tea Fudge

**Maddie** I love it when my friend Cerise joins me for tea parties because she always brings the fairy best sweet treats in her basket! Once she brought this delicious fudge, and now no one can get enough!

## Ingredients

- 1 14-ounce can of sweetened condensed milk
- 6 green tea tea bags
- 1 teaspoon baking soda
- 2½ cups of white chocolate chips

## Directions

1. Line an 8-inch square pan with aluminum foil, and cover it with nonstick spray.

2. Heat the sweetened condensed milk on a stove, but don't let it boil.

3. Soak the tea bags in water, and steep them in the milk for about five minutes. Remove the tea bags.

4. Whisk the baking soda into the milk.

5. Adding the white chocolate chips a half cup at a time, whisk the mixture until the white chocolate has melted.

6. Once all the white chocolate has been added and melted, pour the mixture into the square pan and smooth out the surface.

7. Place the pan in the refrigerator. Let it set for at least three hours.

8. When you're ready to serve it, remove the fudge from the pan and cut it into bite-size pieces.

# Babbling Drinks

Maddie

I've come up with a few refreshing flavors of fizzy ice water that I like to have along with tea in case my friends want something else to wash down their food with. Sometimes I'll make a glass pitcher of one of these drinks, but these recipes are by the glass.

## Berry Fine

This is my go-to crowd-pleaser. Put a handful of raspberries and a handful of mint into a glass. Use the back of a spoon to mash them together a little. Fill half the glass with ice, and add sparkling water, leaving about two inches at the top. Then throw in another handful of raspberries.

## Apple with a Twist

You can't go wrong with serving apple-flavored anything to the Fairest of the Halls. Fill about a quarter of the glass with apple juice, then add ice, filling about half the glass. Pour in the sparkling water, then add about a tablespoon of lime juice (that's the *twist* part!).

# Cerise Cherry Mint

**D**id you know that Cerise's name is a color? And that color happens to be the shade of this drink! Put a small handful of mint into a glass. Use the back of a spoon to mash it a little at the bottom of the glass. Throw in three maraschino cherries. Fill half the glass with ice, and add sparkling water, leaving about an inch at the top. Add about two tablespoons of grenadine to give the drink that cerise colo⬤

## Splin⬤

**C**edar⬤ ⬤t her wooden skin getting all dried out. My cuc⬤ ⬤atermelon drink is the perfect solution. Put half a cup of seedless watermelon and a quarter cup of cucumber slices into a glass, along with a handful of mint. Use the back of a spoon to mash everything together a little. Add some ice and sparkling water.

# Riddlish Contest!

Maddie

Sometimes when I see a confused head tilt from my friends, I know I've accidentally slipped into Riddlish, which is our language back in Wonderland. It might sound like nonsense, but it's not! Ask my friend Raven! She's starting to understand me, so it can't be that hard!

Raven

Maddie's right! It's not that difficult once you start trying! There is no word-for-word translation from English to Riddlish. As the name suggests, Riddlish is made up of riddles. It uses rhymes, clues, and metaphors—kind of like poetry! Maddie says this a lot: "Smiles and laughs, over the moon, the rabbit's clock winds down too soon!" What do you think it means? If you guessed "We're having so much fun and I don't want the party to end," then you're one step closer to being able to understand Maddie!

Come up with some sentences that you and your friends translate into Riddlish. Start with the sentence you want to translate—then think of words or phrases that can stand in for each part of the sentence. Then write the best translation below.

---

---

---

---

---

---

---

---

### EXAMPLES OF WORDS TRANSLATED INTO RIDDLISH:

GO = green light

BIRD = wings

BLUE = feeling less than your best

FRIEND = a nonpoisonous apple

# Hexcellent Hats

Apple

What's a hat-tastic tea party without a fun, fanciful tea hat? Maddie's Hat of Many Things is one of a kind, but you and your guests can also have something just as unique! You can choose to either put these together ahead of time for your guests or make it a party activity—that way, your friends can design their own!

## Tiny Tea Top Hat:

- ♥ paper in various colors or patterns
- ♥ scissors
- ♥ tape

❶ Cut out a circle from a piece of paper. This is the base of your hat.

❷ Decide how tall you want your hat to be. Cut out a long strip of paper that width.

❸ Curl the strip to form a circle and tape it to the base.

❹ Turn it over and trace the small circle. Cut out the circle and tape it on to form the top!

❺ Attach the hat to a headband, or just pin it into your hair!

1

2

3

4

TIP: Decorate the pieces of paper with markers or crayons before assembling your hat!

35

# Lizzie Hearts
## Card Game

In Wonderland, our daily tea at the castle included a good game of croquet. If you don't have a croquet set, you can still pay homage to my home with this card game.

*Lizzie*

> **THIS GAME IS JUST LIKE CRAZY EIGHTS, ONLY THE QUEENS ARE WILD, NOT THE EIGHTS! HERE'S HOW YOU PLAY:**

Each player gets eight cards. The object of the game is to get rid of all your cards. The remaining cards are stacked facedown in the center. To start the game, take the top card and put it face-up beside the deck. If you have a card that is either the same suit (club, spade, heart, diamond) or value, you can put that card on top of the first card. If you don't, you have to take a card from the facedown deck. When that deck runs out of cards, you will have to pass your turn. When you play a queen, you will call out the suit you want the next player to put down.

# OFF WITH YOUR HEAD!

When you put down your last card, you have to shout OFF WITH YOUR HEAD to win!

# Teatime Etiquette Game!

We don't really have tea parties in Hood Hollow. So when I went to my first tea party here at Ever After High, my friends had to teach me all about proper tea etiquette. It was not fairy hexciting, and I could barely hocus focus! But if you turn learning the do's and don'ts for teatime into a game, your BFFAs will have a total ball!

*Cerise*

Write each of the etiquette points on the next page on a slip of paper and put them into a hat. Have a poster board and a marker nearby, or a notepad everyone can see. Taking turns, one person picks a slip and draws what's written on it until someone guesses it correctly. Whoever guesses the most correctly wins.

# Etiquette Points:

- When you **sit down**, put your napkin in your lap.

- If you leave the table, place your napkin on your chair, not the table.

- Stir your tea gently, not wildly.

- When you **stir** your tea, the teaspoon should not hit the cup.

- Your teaspoon goes in the saucer to the right of your cup.

- Pour the tea into your cup before you add milk, sugar, or lemon.

- Don't speak with your mouth full.

- Take small bites of your food.

- The teacup handle should point to the right.

- The fork is placed to the left of the plate.

- The spoon is placed to the right of the plate.

# Tea Teaser

## Gift Bags

Apple

Everyone knows I like to be prepared so I know what to hexpect. So at my tea parties, I give out what I like to call Tea Teasers! These hat-tastic gift bags give my guests a hint of what the theme of my next tea party will be. It keeps them guessing and stirs up some hexcitement!

At the party before my All Things Apple tea party, each gift bag contained a shiny red apple, a red apple-shaped eraser, an apple cinnamon tea bag, and apple stickers. At that party, I gave out these evil-looking hairbands that had spikes on them, black feather pens, Black Heart black tea bags, and magic mirrors I bought in the Village of Book End that turned the looker's face into a goblin's.

**Q:** Can you guess what the next party was supposed to be?

**A:** Yeah, I was hoping to throw my roomie, Raven, a Be Evil tea party, but she nixed that idea.

Before your party, assemble a gift bag for each of your friends. Decorate some gift bags using markers, stickers, ribbons—whatever you like! Then fill them with treats that will "tease" to what your next tea party's theme will be! Or fill them with cookies like the ones Maddie shares on page 42.

## A Thoughtful Note

Sometimes I have tricks up my sleeve, but I never mean to hurt other people's feelings, especially at my tea parties. I love having all my guests there, so I make sure to send thank-you notes afterward. I know I always appreciate getting these from my friends. Here's one that I sent recently:

Dear Lizzie Hearts,

Thank you so much for coming to my tea party. I hope I didn't get carried away with my pranks, and I'm glad you found it fairy funny that I replaced the sugar for the tea with salt!

Let's have another hat-tastic tea party soon! It was a wonderlandiful time!

Friends until The End,
Kitty Cheshire

# Tea Bag Sweet Treat

Maddie

I slip these chocolate-covered tea bag cookies into my gift bags to remind my BFFAs of our hexcellent teatime—and to encourage them to visit my father's Tea Shoppe! Here is my recipe. If you have your own favorite sugar cookie recipe, you can make the dough and skip to "Directions, Chapter 2."

## Ingredients

- ♥ 2¼ cups of all-purpose flour
- ♥ 1 teaspoon of baking soda
- ♥ ½ teaspoon of baking powder
- ♥ 1 cup of butter, melted
- ♥ 1½ cups of white sugar
- ♥ 1 egg
- ♥ 1 teaspoon of vanilla extract
- ♥ 1 cup semisweet chocolate chips

## Directions, Chapter 1

1. Preheat the oven to 375 degrees Fahrenheit, and line baking sheets with aluminum foil.

2. In a small bowl, mix the flour, baking soda, and baking powder.

3. In a large bowl, cream together the butter and sugar until the mixture is smooth.

4. Beat in the egg and vanilla.

5. Add the dry ingredients to the large bowl a little at a time.

# Directions, Chapter 2

1. On a lightly floured board or clean counter, roll out the dough until it is about an eighth of an inch thick.

2. Using a knife, carefully cut the dough into rectangles about one inch by three inches.

3. Cut triangles off the corners on one of the short sides so that the dough looks like a tea bag.

4. Using a drinking straw, poke a hole between the cut corners of the "tea bag."

5. Place these "tea bags" on the baking sheets. Bake for eight minutes, or until lightly golden.

6. Let the cookie sheets cool completely.

# Directions, Chapter 3

1. When the cookies have cooled, put the chocolate chips in a microwave-safe bowl and microwave it thirty seconds at a time, stirring frequently, until the chocolate is completely melted.

2. Dip each cookie one-third of the way. Set the cookie on a parchment-lined baking sheet or a wire rack to dry.

3. When the cookies have dried, slip a pretty ribbon through the hole of the "tea bag" and tie the ends together.

4. You can put these cookies into plastic bags and tie the bags with other ribbons to dress them up!

TIPS: I like to personalize these cookie presents for my friends:

- For Apple's cookie, I put on some red sprinkles before the chocolate completely dried.
- For Kitty's cookie, I tied a sprig of lavender, her fairy favorite color, to the bag.
- For Cerise's cookie, I melted a few white chocolate chips, then painted a white streak onto the brown chocolate. It looked just like the white streaks in her brown hair!
- For Cedar's cookie, I made a tea bag cookie puppet! I glued together two toothpicks into a cross. Then, instead of a ribbon, I slipped two puppet strings through the hole of the cookie and tied the other ends to each point on the toothpick cross. And then I made the cookie dance!

# Your Tea Party's Story

Now that we've shown you how hat-tastic our tea parties are, it's your turn to plan your own soiree! Jot down your ideas here!

Cedar

Fairytale inspiration:

My tea party theme is:

My tea party colors are:

Snack and drink ideas:

_____

_____

_____

_____

_____

Activity ideas:

_____

_____

_____

_____

Gift bag ideas:

_____

_____

_____

_____

# Your Epic Invite

Maddie

Have you been inspired by our invitations?
Design your own here!